≫ *For Lyall* ≪

VIKING

Published by the Penguin Group

Penguin Young Readers Group, 345 Hudson Street, New York, New York 10014, U.S.A.

Penguin Group (Canada), 90 Eglinton Avenue East, Suite 700, Toronto, Ontario, Canada M4P 2Y3
(a division of Pearson Penguin Canada Inc.)

Penguin Books Ltd, 80 Strand, London WC2R 0RL, England

Penguin Ireland, 25 St Stephen's Green, Dublin 2, Ireland (a division of Penguin Books Ltd)

Penguin Group (Australia), 250 Camberwell Road, Camberwell, Victoria 3124, Australia
(a division of Pearson Australia Group Pty Ltd)

Penguin Books India Pvt Ltd, 11 Community Centre, Panchsheel Park, New Delhi – 110 017, India

Penguin Group (NZ), 67 Apollo Drive, Rosedale, Auckland 0632, New Zealand (a division of Pearson New Zealand Ltd.)

Penguin Books (South Africa) (Pty) Ltd, 24 Sturdee Avenue, Rosebank, Johannesburg 2196, South Africa

Penguin Books Ltd, Registered Offices: 80 Strand, London WC2R 0RL, England

First published in the United States of America by Viking, a division of Penguin Young Readers Group, 2012

1 3 5 7 9 10 8 6 4 2

Copyright © Gianna Marino, 2012

All rights reserved

LIBRARY OF CONGRESS CATALOGING-IN-PUBLICATION DATA

Marino, Gianna.

Too tall houses / by Gianna Marino.

p. cm.

Summary: Owl and Rabbit are good friends and neighbors atop a hill, but when Rabbit's garden blocks Owl's view
of the forest Owl builds a higher house, which prevents sunlight from reaching Rabbit's plants.

ISBN 978-0-670-01314-2 (hardcover)

[1. Dwellings—Fiction. 2. Owls—Fiction. 3. Rabbits—Fiction.] I. Title.

PZ7.M33882Too 2012   [E]—dc23   2011048294

Manufactured in China   Set in Ionic   Book design by Nancy Brennan

The illustrations for this book were rendered in gouache and pencil on Fabriano Artistico paper.

E
Marino,
Gianna

TOO TALL HOUSES

GIANNA MARINO

VIKING

An Imprint of Penguin Group (USA) Inc.

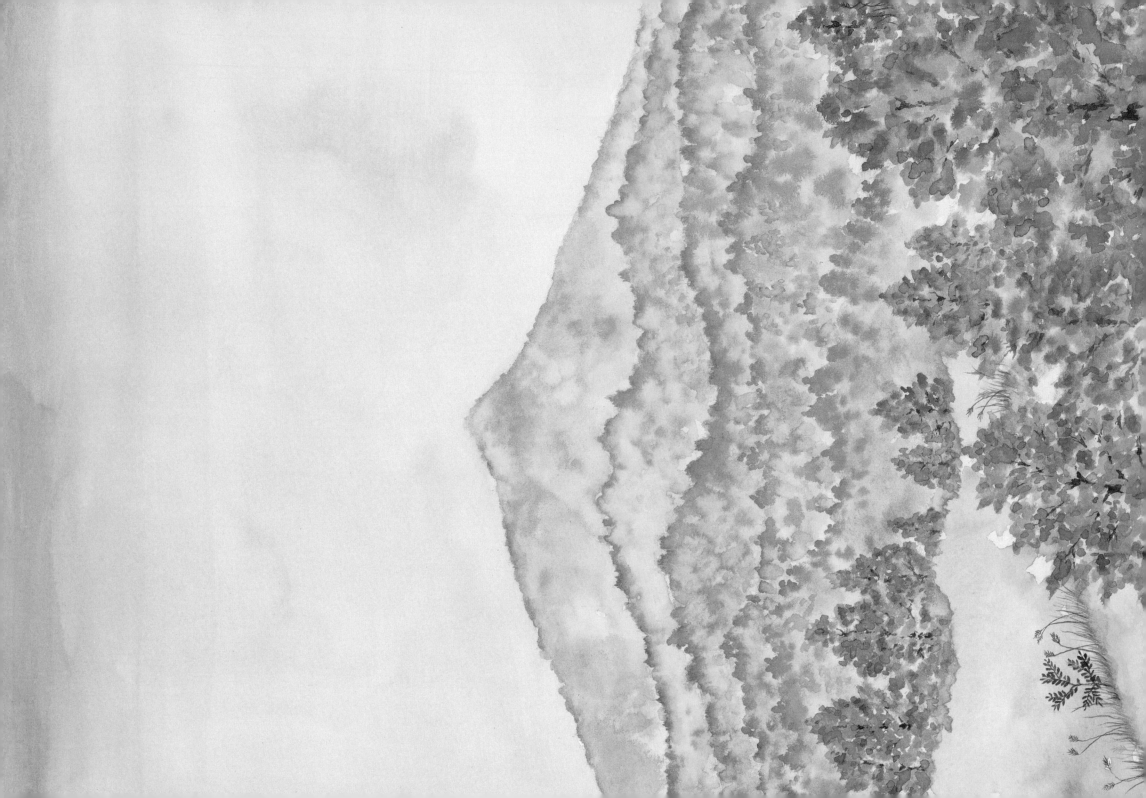

Rabbit and Owl lived in two small houses on top of a hill.

Rabbit liked to grow vegetables in the sun,

and Owl enjoyed the view of the forest.

In the evening, they played under the twilight sky.

They were good neighbors and good friends,

until one day . . .

"Rabbit!" Owl complained.

"Your garden is growing too tall.

I can't see the forest!"

"But what can I do?" replied Rabbit.

"I have to grow my food."

So Owl began to build his house taller.

Rabbit watched and chittered his teeth.

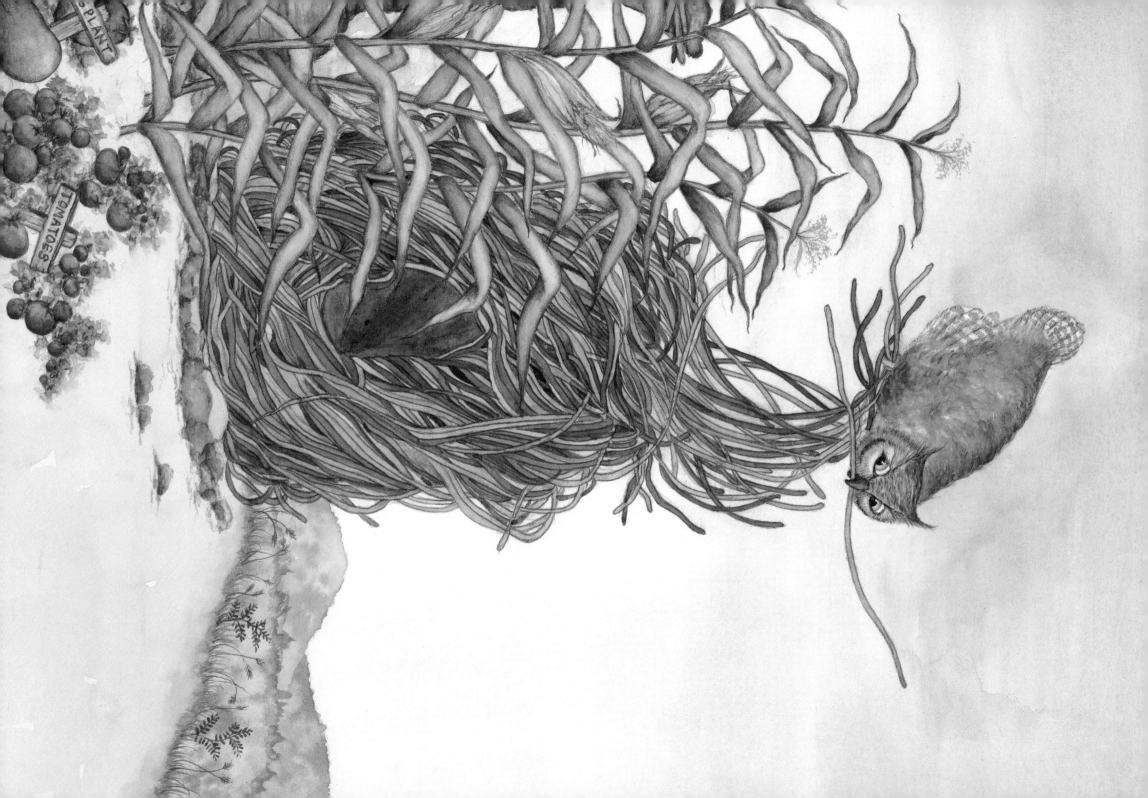

"Owl! Look what you did!
Your house is blocking the sun
from reaching my garden!"

"But I have to see the forest,"
said Owl.

So Rabbit built his house taller, too,

and planted some vegetables on the roof.

But when Rabbit watered his rooftop plants . . .

it made Owl
VERY
angry.

So Owl built his house even taller.

'*I want to be the tallest!*'

yelled Rabbit.

"WHAT?!" screeched Owl.

"You are so far below

me

that

I

can't

hear

you!"

So Rabbit built his house
even taller and put a fence
around his garden.

"Hoo-hoo-who do you think you are?" screeched Owl.

And he went to find more twigs for his house.

And Rabbit went to fetch
more soil for *his* house.

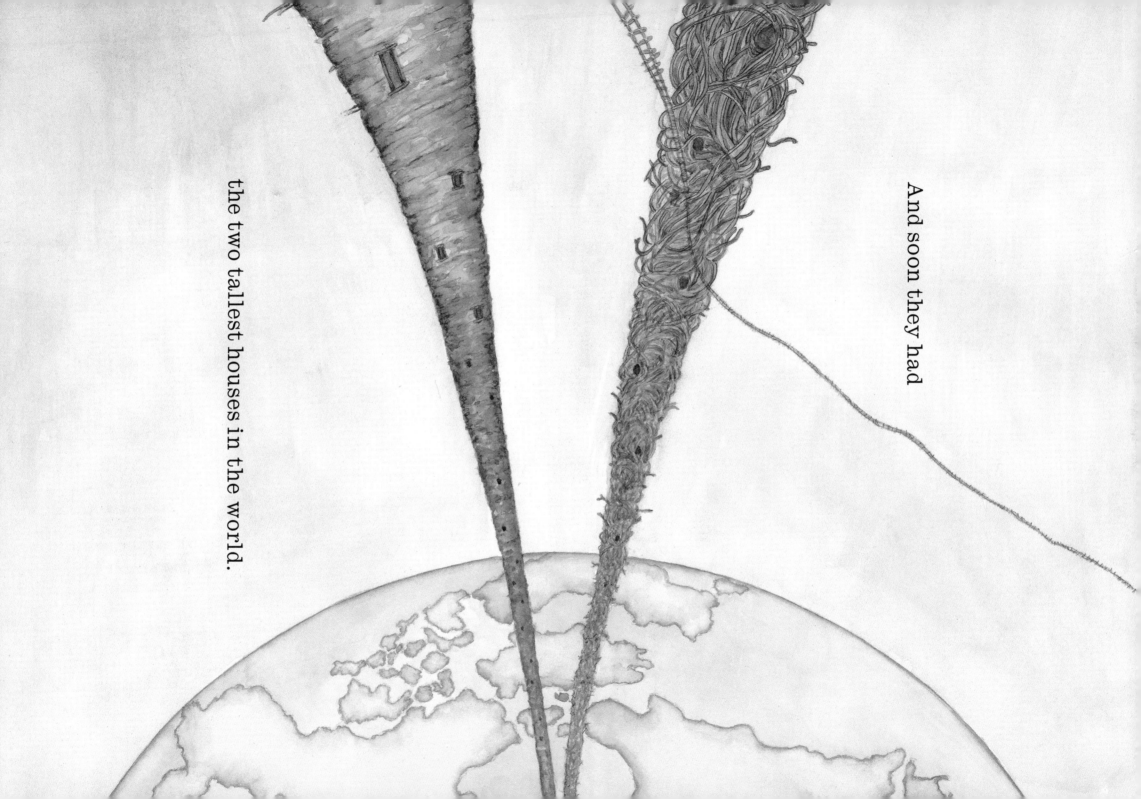

the two tallest houses in the world.

And soon they had

"Owl! I can't carry water up my ladder!" cried Rabbit.

"And I can't see the forest," said Owl.

Way up high,
the wind roared and bellowed,

Whoosh!
Crreeeaakkkkk . . .

and blew the
too tall houses
into the air.

Crack! . . .

Whooosh . . .

"Hold on, Rabbit!"
cried Owl.

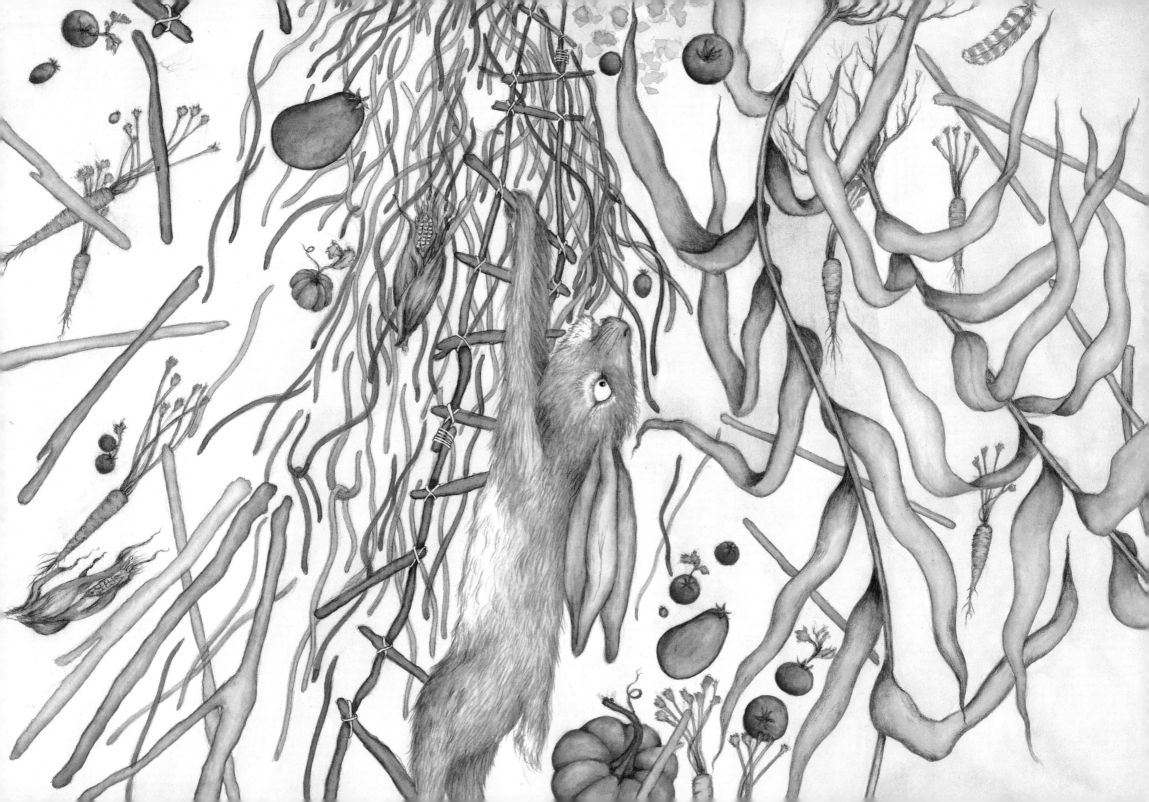

They landed with a *plunk*.

"All I have left is a pile of dirt," moaned Rabbit.

"My house is a bunch of broken twigs," sighed Owl.

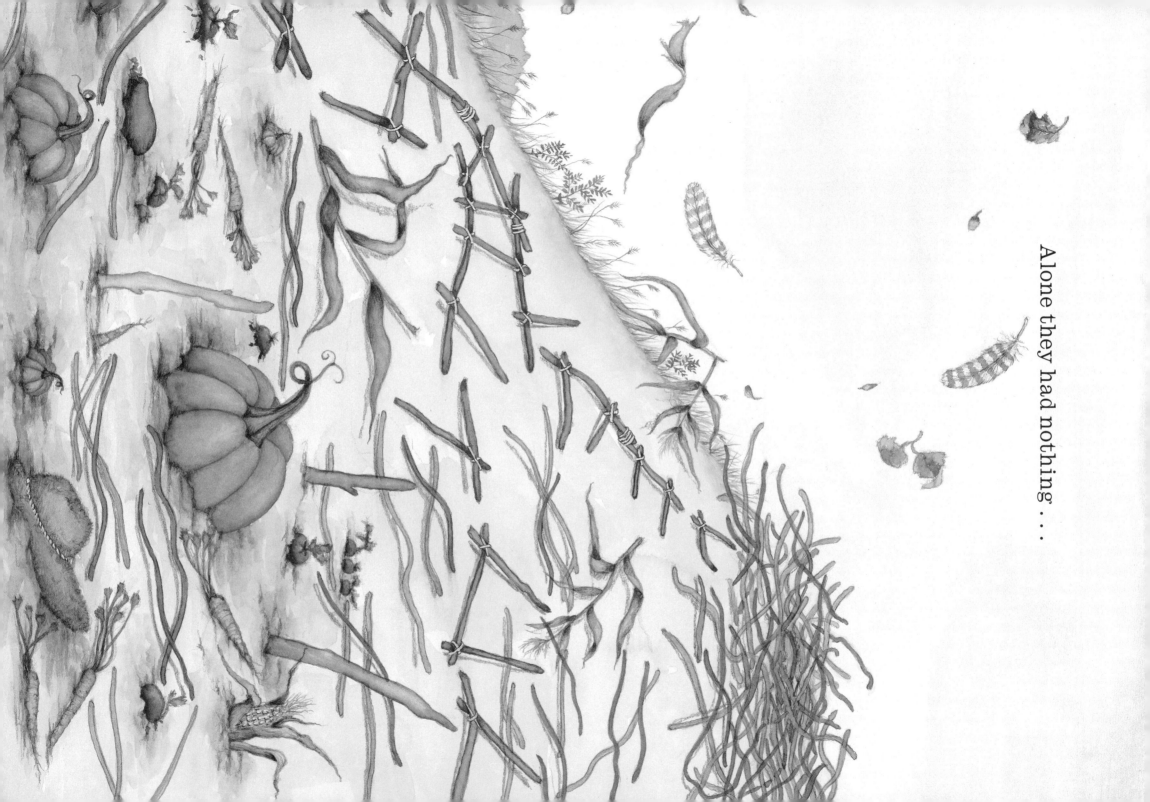

Alone they had nothing . . .

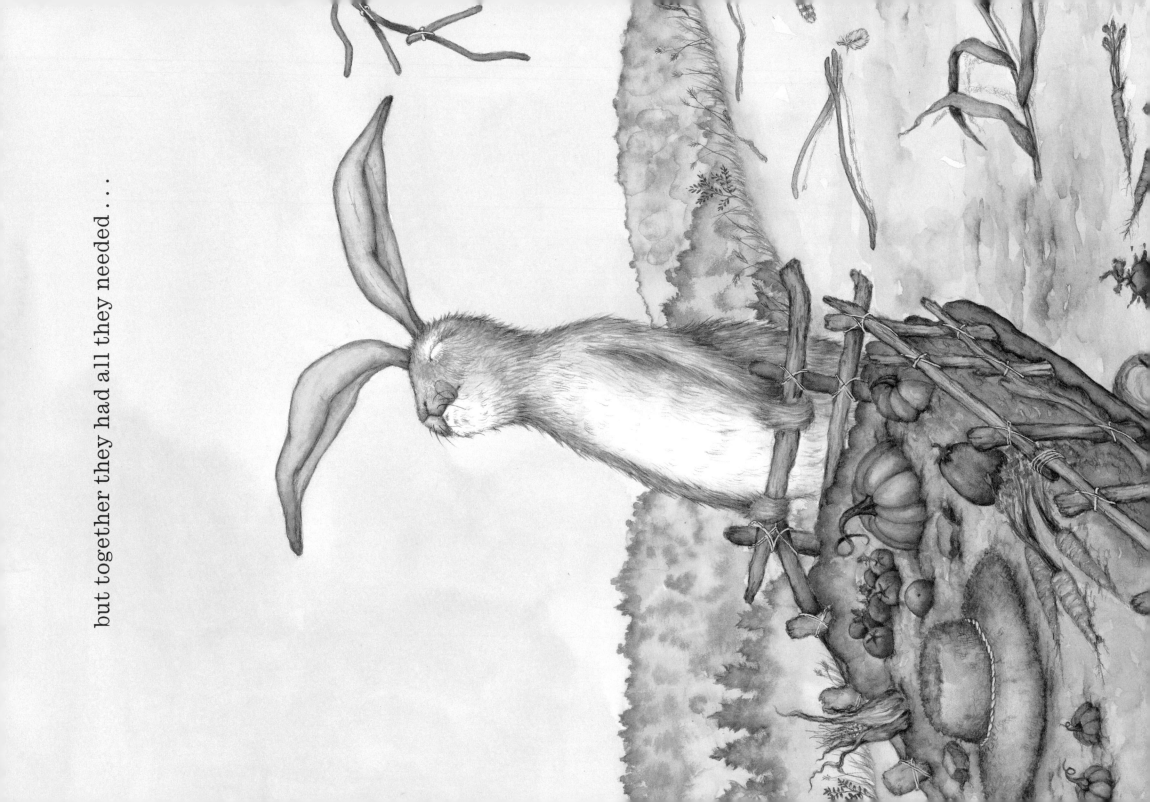

but together they had all they needed . . .

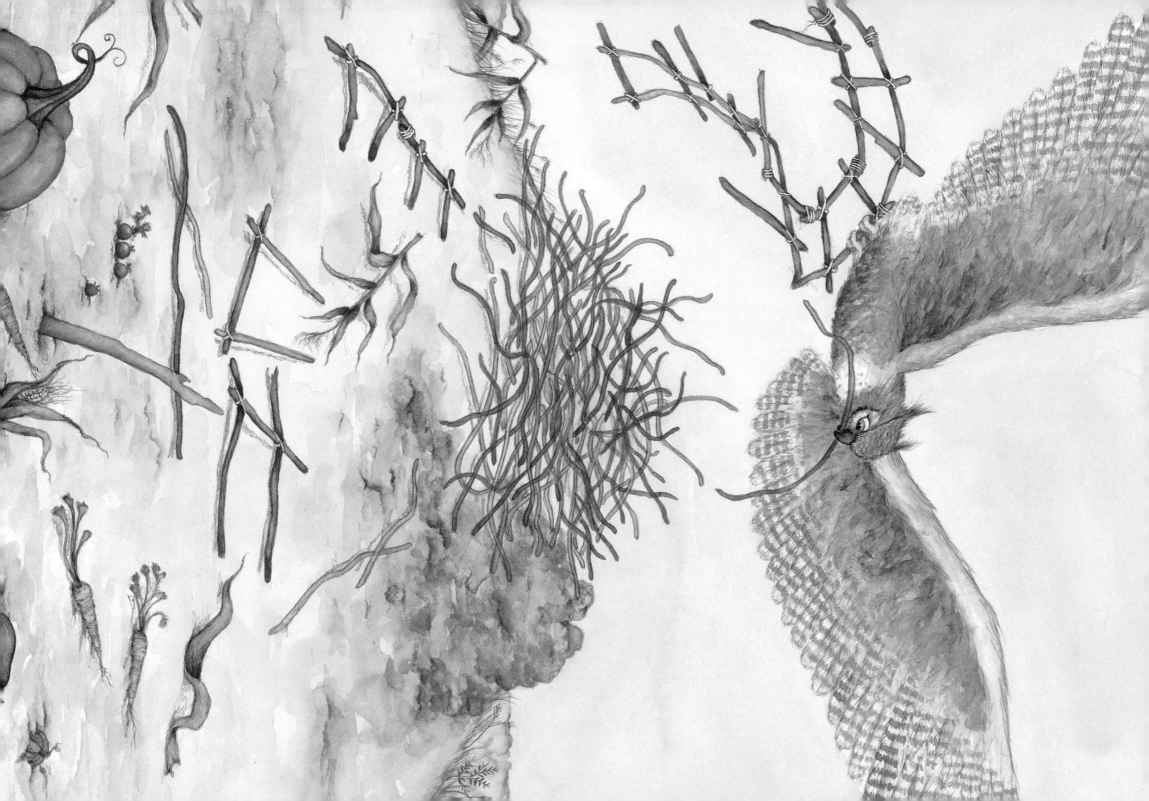

to build one small house.

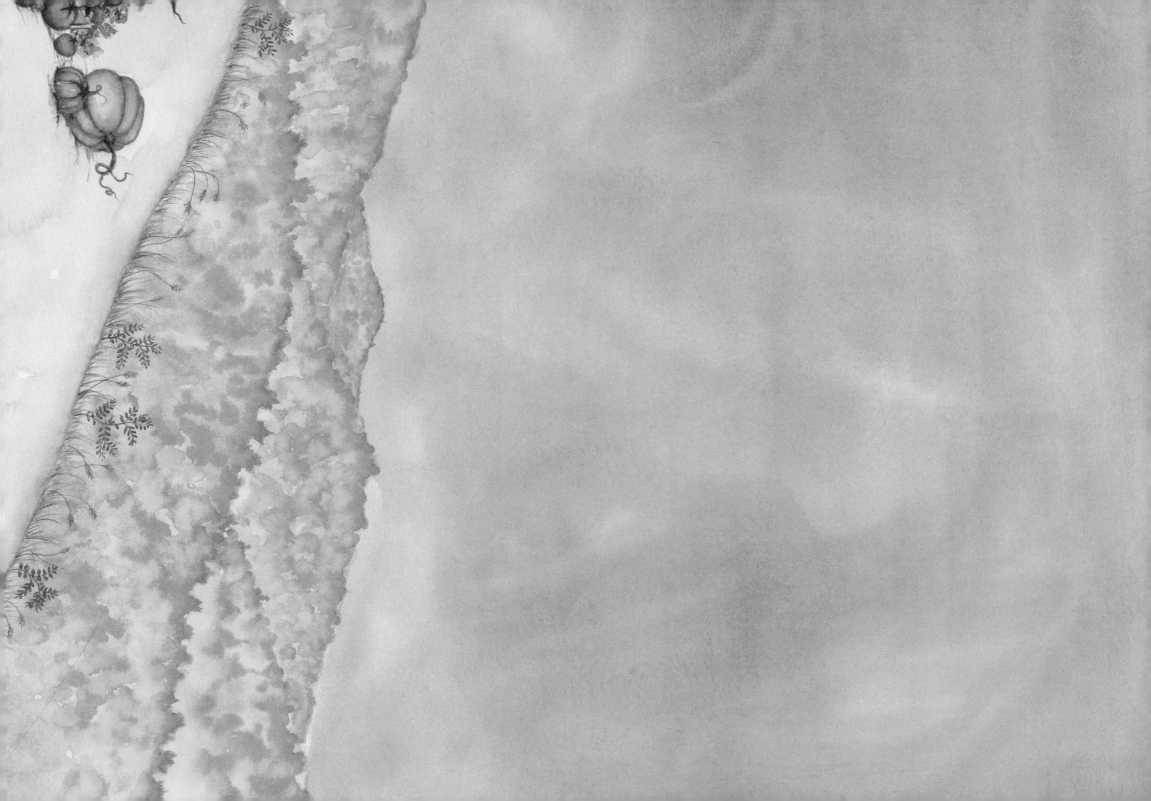